Little Rabbit
Goes to School

HARRY HORSE

PEACHTREE
ATLANTA

For Elliot

Published by
PEACHTREE PUBLISHERS, LTD.
1700 Chattahoochee Avenue
Atlanta, Georgia 30318-2112
www.peachtree-online.com

Text and Illustrations © 2007 by Harry Horse

Illustrations created in pen and ink and watercolor.

First published in Great Britain by Penguin Books in 2004
First United States hardcover edition published in 2004
First United States trade paperback edition published in 2011

Printed in November 2010 by KHL Printing Co Pte Ltd in Singapore
10 9 8 7 6 5 4 (hardcover)
10 9 8 7 6 5 4 3 2 1 (trade paperback)

ISBN 13: 978-1-56145-320-7 / ISBN 10: 1-56145-320-X (hardcover)
ISBN 13: 978-1-56145-574-4 / ISBN 10: 1-56145-574-1 (trade paperback)

Library of Congress Cataloging-in-Publication Data is available from the United States Library of Congress

When Little Rabbit woke up, he knew that it was
a special day. Today was his first day of school.

Little Rabbit got Charlie Horse out of bed. "Come on, Charlie Horse," said Little Rabbit. "You have to go to school."

He brushed Charlie Horse's tail and tied on a red ribbon.

He took Charlie Horse along to show Mama.

"Now we are big," said Little Rabbit proudly. "We are going to school."

"Maybe Charlie Horse should stay at home with me," said Mama.

"I don't think wooden horses go to school."

But Little Rabbit would not listen.
"No, Mama," he said. "Charlie Horse
wants to go to school."

Mama gave Little Rabbit his lunch box and
told him not to open it until lunchtime.
"I won't, Mama," cried Little Rabbit.

Little Rabbit skipped
along after his brothers and sisters.
"Come on, Charlie Horse," said
Little Rabbit. "Don't be late for school."

Soon Charlie Horse needed
to stop for a little rest.

He wanted to open the
lunch box and take a look inside.

But he didn't like the lettuce
sandwiches, so Little Rabbit
had to eat them. And he
didn't like the carrot cakes, so
Little Rabbit had to eat them too.

"Come on, Little Rabbit!"
called his brothers and sisters.
"We'll be late for school."
"It's Charlie Horse's fault! He's making
me late!" said Little Rabbit. "Come on,
Charlie Horse, stop making me late."

The school was much bigger than Little Rabbit thought it would be. His new teacher, Miss Morag, was very pleased to see him. She liked Charlie Horse.

Miss Morag showed Little Rabbit his new classroom.
He was very shy. Everybody turned to look at him
and Charlie Horse.

"This is Little Rabbit," said Miss Morag.

Miss Morag read them a story called
The Bad Rabbits and even though it was a
good story, Little Rabbit could not keep
Charlie Horse still.

Charlie Horse wanted to gallop
over the fields.

He galloped across Benjamin...

he galloped over Rachel...

he even galloped over Miss Morag's shoes. Little Rabbit pulled him back.

Miss Morag let Charlie Horse rest on her desk
while Little Rabbit painted a picture.

After painting, they learned a song. It was called,
"If You Need a Friend Just Whistle."
Little Rabbit liked singing. Miss Morag said
he was a good whistler too.

But she didn't like it when Charlie Horse
jumped off the table and danced.
She made Charlie Horse
sit in the corner for the
rest of the song.

Next they made little cakes. But Charlie Horse
was naughty and jumped into the cake batter.

Miss Morag did not like Charlie Horse in the cake batter.
She had to give him a bath.

Then it was time for recess.
The rabbits played games.
They scampered and hopped in the
meadow, they dug holes, and they
chased each other through
the long grass.

But Little Rabbit played alone with Charlie Horse.
He did not share him with Benjamin.
He did not let Rachel play with him either.
"Charlie Horse does not want to play
with you," said Little Rabbit.

Miss Morag rang the bell for lunch. All the rabbits
opened their lunch boxes. But when Little Rabbit looked
for his, he began to cry.

"What's the matter, Little Rabbit?"
asked Miss Morag.

"Somebody has eaten my lunch," cried
Little Rabbit, "and now I have none."

"You can have some of mine," said Benjamin.
"Don't cry, Little Rabbit. You can have
some of mine too," said Rachel.
Little Rabbit shared lunch
with his new friends.

When they'd finished, he let them play with Charlie Horse.
"Charlie Horse likes you best," said Little Rabbit.

After lunch, Miss Morag took some of the little rabbits on a nature walk. Charlie Horse came along too.

"Don't you want to leave Charlie Horse behind?" said the teacher.

"No, Miss Morag," said Little Rabbit. "Charlie Horse likes nature walks too."

On the way, Charlie Horse found a beautiful flower.

Miss Morag would like that flower, thought Little Rabbit.

So he let go of Benjamin's hand and followed Charlie Horse instead.

"Look what we found, Miss Morag!" said Little Rabbit.

But when he looked round, nobody was there.

"Where is everybody?" cried Little Rabbit.

Even with Charlie Horse, he felt all alone.

Little Rabbit dragged Charlie Horse along a path in the woods.

He lost a shoe.

His coat got caught
on a prickle bush.

"This is all your fault, Charlie Horse,"
said Little Rabbit. "You made me lose my way.
Now I'll never find my way back."

Then Little Rabbit remembered the song that
Miss Morag had taught the class that morning.
"If you need a friend, just whistle," sang Little Rabbit.
His song rang out in the dark woods.

Just as he began to whistle,
he heard Miss Morag calling him.

Little Rabbit ran.

Miss Morag picked him up
and they all went back to school.

When they got back to school, Mama and Papa were already waiting for him, ready to go home.

And on the way, Little Rabbit told them all about school and, best of all, his new friends.

"I can't wait to go to school again," said Little Rabbit, "but tomorrow Charlie Horse can stay at home with you, Mama. He's too naughty for school."

"What a good idea," said Mama.